Magic Ballerina

Rosa and the **Magic Moonstone**

AND

Holly and the **Dancing Cat**

Welcome to the world of Enchantia!

I have always loved to dance. The captivating music and wonderful stories of ballet are so inspiring. So come with me and let's follow Rosa and Holly on their magical adventures in Enchantia, where the stories of dance will take you on a very special journey.

[signature]

p.s. Turn to the end of each story to learn a special dance step from me...

Special thanks to
Linda Chapman, Katie May
and Nellie Ryan

Rosa and the Magic Moonstone first published in paperback in Great Britain by
HarperCollins Children's Books in 2009
Holly and the Dancing Cat first published in paperback in Great Britain by
HarperCollins Children's Books in 2009
Published together in this two-in-one edition in 2011
HarperCollins Children's Books is a division of HarperCollins Publishers Ltd,
77–85 Fulham Palace Road, Hammersmith, London W6 8JB

The HarperCollins website address is
www.harpercollins.co.uk

1

ISBN 978-0-00-741442-0

Printed and bound in England by
Clays Ltd, St Ives plc

Magic Ballerina™

Rosa and the Magic Moonstone

Darcey Bussell

HarperCollins *Children's Books*

To Phoebe and Zoe, as they are the inspiration behind Magic Ballerina.

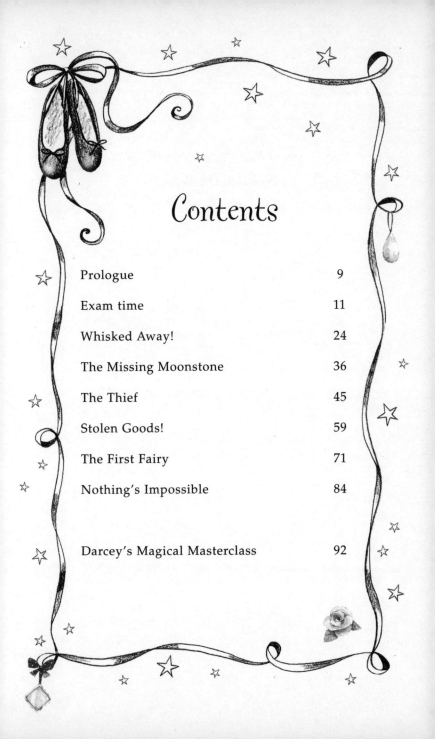

Contents

Prologue

*In the soft, pale light, the girl stood
with her head bent and her hands
held lightly in front of her.
There was a moment's silence and then
the first notes of the music began.
For as long as the girl could remember
music had seemed to tell her of
another world – a magical, exciting
world – that lay far, far away.
She always felt if she could just
close her eyes and lose herself,
then she would get there.
Maybe this time. As the music
swirled inside her, she swept
her arms above her head, rose on to
her toes and began to dance…*

Exam Time

The group of girls crowded into the changing rooms, chattering loudly.

"I can't believe we're going to be doing the exam *tomorrow*!" Olivia said.

"I know," replied Rebecca. "I'm really nervous."

"I'm scared stiff," agreed Asha.

Rosa Maitland looked at her friends in

surprise. "But why?" She twirled round
before sitting down and starting to untie
the ribbons on her red ballet shoes. "I'm
looking forward to it."

Rosa loved
dancing in front
of people. She
didn't care
whether it was
her teacher,
Madame Za-Za,
an audience at a
theatre or an
examiner in the ballet studio. She just loved
to dance!

"But what if we go wrong?" said Olivia.
"What if we forget everything?"

"Why would we?" Rosa said. "We're just doing the same exercises we do every lesson for Madame Za-Za. Stop worrying about it."

She got changed out of her leotard and after saying goodbye to Olivia and the others, she headed home. Rosa only lived around the corner. As she let herself into the house, her mum came into the hall in her wheelchair. Mrs Maitland had once been a ballerina, but then a car accident had ended her career. She still loved ballet, though, and often helped Rosa.

"How did the exam practice go?" she asked.

"Great." Rosa smiled as she remembered.

"It was cool dancing with a proper pianist playing and Madame Za-Za said I did my dances really well."

Mrs Maitland nodded. "How about your *barre* work?"

"Easy peasy!" grinned Rosa. She took hold of the kitchen door handle with her left hand and raised her leg to the *retiré* position,

bringing her right arm above her head, just like she would have to do in the exam. "Everyone else is really nervous, but I don't know why. I'm sure we're all going to pass."

Her mum looked anxious. "Rosa, it's really great you're not worried about the exam, but remember things can go wrong. If they do you must just keep on going and not give up. Don't expect to get everything right."

Rosa smiled confidently. "I'll be fine!" She danced into the kitchen. "What's for tea, Mum?"

"Pasta," said Mrs Maitland, following her. "Will you set the table, please, while I heat the sauce?"

Rosa nodded and started to get the

cutlery out. "What mark do you think I'll get for the exam?" she wondered.

Her mum smiled. "I don't know, sweetheart. But so long as you try your hardest, I'll be proud of you."

In bed that night, Rosa ran through the exercises she was going to have to do in her exam. Madame Za-Za had explained that the girls would go in groups of four. First they would do *barre* work, like they did every week in class, then they would go into the centre of the studio and do some more exercises there. After that they would take it in turns to do a set dance and then they had character work to do. Rosa had

practised over and over again. What mark
would she get? The highest grade you could
get was an A, which was also called
distinction, and then it went B for merit, C
for pass and if you didn't get any of those
you failed. She really hoped she would
do well.

She reached out to turn her bedside light
off. As she did so, her eyes fell on the red
ballet shoes hanging at the
end of her bed. She
smiled. They were her
most precious things in
the whole world. They were
made of soft red leather and fitted her feet
perfectly, but that wasn't why they were so
special. They were special because they

were magic! Sometimes they would start to sparkle and glow and then they would whisk her off to Enchantia, a magic land where all the characters from the different ballets lived. Rosa had been on some brilliant adventures there already. She had met the King and Queen, made friends with a fairy called Nutmeg and her older sister, Sugar, the Sugar Plum Fairy. She had come up against some pretty horrible characters too – like King Rat and the Wicked Fairy. But most of the people who lived in Enchantia were really nice.

Rosa snuggled down under her duvet. She bet no one in Enchantia had to do exams. When would she go there again?

She hugged her arms around herself. She hoped it would be soon!

In the morning, Rosa arrived at the ballet school early. She got changed into her leotard and smoothed her wavy blonde hair back into a neat bun. She was beginning to feel slightly nervous. She was ready before the other girls arrived, warming up by doing *pliés*, holding lightly on to one of the sinks as if it was the *barre*.

"Hi," Olivia called over. Her face was pale and her eyes looked wide and frightened.

Rosa saw her fingers shaking as she started to pull down the zip on her coat.

"It'll be OK," Rosa told her. She stretched her left foot out in front of her and lifted it quickly upwards as she practised a *grande battement*.

Back still, knees tight… the things to remember ran through her head as she lowered her foot slowly to the floor.

"I feel like I'm going to be sick," said Olivia.

"Me too," said Rebecca, sitting down beside her.

"And me," said Asha, looking alarmed. "What happens if we *are* sick in the exam?"

As she spoke the door opened and Madame Za-Za came in. As usual, the ballet teacher was wearing a long ballet skirt, bangles and necklaces. Her greying hair

was tied back in a bun. She caught Asha's words. "You will not be sick, Asha," she said in her slight Russian accent. She smiled. "You will go into the exam room and perform your very best. I am sure all of you are going to make me proud. Now, when you're ready, please come to studio two and start to warm up."

Rosa hurried eagerly through the door.

Half an hour later, Rosa stood with Olivia, Asha and Rebecca in the corridor, waiting for Madame Za-Za to tell them they could go into the studio where the examiner was. They were going to be the first group in. Rosa was glad. She wanted to get started. Each of the four girls had a different

coloured ribbon pinned to her chest so the examiner would know who was who. Each of them was also holding the skirts and shoes they would need for their character work at the end.

"Does my hair look OK?" Rosa asked Olivia.

Olivia nodded. "How about mine?"

"You look great!" Rosa squeezed her hand. "Good luck!"

"You too!" Olivia said nervously.

Madame Za-Za held the door open. A bell rang inside the room. "In you go, girls."

Taking a deep breath, Rosa followed Asha, Rebecca and Olivia into the studio. The exam was about to begin!

Whisked Away!

Rosa and the other girls put down their
shoes and skirts at the side of the room
and curtsied to the examiner who was
beside a small table. The examiner, a
small slim woman, smiled and looked at
their ribbons. "Good morning, girls. Let
me just check I have your names and
colours right. Asha – pink, Rebecca – blue,

Olivia – yellow and Rosa – white?"

They all nodded.

"Excellent. Take your places at the *barre*, please."

As they began to go through their exercises, Rosa felt happy and relaxed. She remembered to keep her back straight, her chin up, her hips still and her movements smooth. She wished she could look over at the others and see how they were doing, but she was concentrating too hard. She enjoyed stretching every muscle as much as she could, keeping her arm movements flowing and graceful.

After working at the *barre* they went to the centre of the studio. The first few exercises went well. *I'm really doing OK,*

Rosa thought, as they got ready to start their pirouette exercises. *I wonder what mark I'll get. Mum would be so pleased if I...*

Suddenly she realised that she had been distracted and the examiner had told them all to start. The others were already turning. She quickly tried to join in, but wobbled badly as she came to a stop. She glanced at the examiner, hoping she hadn't noticed, but the examiner was looking directly at her. Rosa blushed. Oh no. She'd really messed that exercise up!

The next exercise was *changements* – jumps where their feet swapped position in the air. Usually Rosa could do them easily but, feeling flustered still, she lost her balance. It went from bad to worse. In

every exercise she seemed
to make a mistake and
the harder she tried,
the worse it got. Her
arms and legs felt
wrong, her jumps
felt rushed and her
landings were
unbalanced. By the
time they finished
working in the centre,
Rosa's cheeks were blazing.
She didn't think she had ever done her
exercises so badly.

Her eyes prickled with tears as she lined
up with the others at one end of the studio
for the set dance. *I'm going to fail for sure,*

she thought, brushing away her tears. The music started and Asha began. She danced lightly across the floor, her elegance making Rosa feel worse than ever.

I'm not going to get a distinction or a merit. I'm not even going to pass. Mum's going to be

so upset with me and what's Madame Za-Za going to say? Maybe she'll make me go down to a different class!

It was impossible. She'd never pass. She didn't want to do the set dance and the character work now. Wild ideas filled her head. Maybe she should just say she was sick and leave. She just wanted to run out of the room.

Asha finished the dance and Rebecca began.

Suddenly Rosa's feet started to tingle. She glanced down at her shoes. They were glowing! She caught her breath. She must be about to go to Enchantia! Luckily she knew that not even a second would pass in the real world while she was away in the magic land, so no one in the room would notice she had gone.

A rainbow of bright colours started to swirl around her and the next minute she felt herself lifted into the air and whisked away.

Rosa spun round and round until the magic gently lowered her down. She blinked as the swirl of colours faded. She was sitting in an empty theatre. It was dark and the heavy curtains were drawn across the stage.

She rubbed a couple of half-dry tears from her cheeks, trying to get her head round the fact that she wasn't in the exam room any more. Where was she? She knew she must be in Enchantia, but she'd landed in the wood before, never in this theatre.

Just then the air filled with music and the curtains started to open, revealing a brightly-lit stage. A girl in a nightdress danced on. Maybe it's Clara from *The Nutcracker*, thought Rosa, wondering what was happening. But then she saw that the girl wasn't holding a nutcracker doll, she was holding a pumpkin! She was followed by a group of soldiers who looked like they were also from *The Nutcracker*. They were fighting a group of dancing giant sweets. *But in the ballet they fight an army of mice,* thought Rosa.

Before she had time to say anything, the soldiers had danced off the stage and a girl in rags had come on. *Cinderella!* thought Rosa. A beautiful fairy spun on after her. But it wasn't Cinderella's Fairy Godmother, it was Sugar, the Sugar Plum Fairy! Two more people followed them. They were dancing a *pas de deux*. One of them was a

beautiful girl with long dark hair who looked like Sleeping Beauty. Rosa stared. Sleeping Beauty wasn't dancing with her handsome prince, though, instead she was dancing with a surprised-looking Puss in Boots!

What's going on? Rosa wondered. *All the ballets seem to be completely mixed up!*

The curtain started to close. Rosa jumped to her feet. "Wait!" she called. She hurried out of the row of seats. But the curtains had shut.

Rosa hesitated, trying to decide what she should do when suddenly there was a tinkling of music and a fairy with dark hair wearing a pale brown and pink tutu danced on to the stage, travelling and turning with every step.

"Nutmeg!" cried Rosa, recognising her friend. She ran down the aisle to the stage. "Nutmeg! It's you!"

"Oh, Rosa!" the fairy stopped in perfect balance, her arms out to the sides. "I'm so glad you're here! We're in trouble again."

Rosa knew the red shoes only brought her to Enchantia when there was a problem to be solved. "Why?"

Nutmeg took a deep breath. "It's a long story. Come and sit down and I'll explain…"

The Missing Moonstone

Rosa and Nutmeg sat down on the edge of the stage. "So, what's happening, Nutmeg?" asked Rosa.

"King Tristan's magical moonstone ring has been stolen," replied Nutmeg. "It's a very special ring. It was given to him by the First Fairy of Enchantia, the fairy who was here when all the ballets were created. The

moonstone keeps all the stories in order and makes them work as they should. Since it's been missing none of the ballets have been right."

"I saw everything going wrong," said Rosa. "I couldn't work out what was happening."

"It's awful," said Nutmeg. "Everything's all mixed up."

"Why don't you just get the ring back?" asked Rosa. "Then everything would be all right again."

"It's not that simple," Nutmeg sighed. "We don't know who stole it, you see. Someone pretending to be a magical jeweller tricked the ring from the King. He said he had been sent by the First Fairy to clean it. As soon as he had the ring in his hands he vanished. Look. I can show you."

Nutmeg stood up and touched her wand to the ground. A pale pink mist appeared.

Rosa gasped as she saw a picture start to form inside it! It showed King Tristan in the courtyard of the Royal Palace. He was talking to a figure wrapped in a black cloak. As Rosa watched, the King took a gold ring with a sparkling white stone off his finger. He handed it to the cloaked figure. Then the figure spun round and vanished in a bright flash of light.

Rosa frowned when she caught sight of something poking out from underneath the black cloak – a long thin tail. It was only there for a second before it vanished.

"Did you see that?" she cried as Nutmeg touched the mist and it cleared.

"What?" asked Nutmeg.

"There was a tail sticking out from under the cloak!"

"Let me see." Nutmeg tapped the floor again and the mist reappeared. Within seconds she and Rosa were watching the vision repeating itself. This time Nutmeg gasped too. "You're right!"

They looked at each other.

"There's only one person that can be," said Rosa. "It must be King Rat! He must have taken the ring!"

"But why?" said Nutmeg.

"There's only one way to find out," replied Rosa bravely. "Let's go to his castle and see."

"But the mouse guards are so scary, and what if King Rat finds us," Nutmeg protested. "You know how much he hates people who dance and he doesn't like us at all after we stopped his last wicked plan."

"It doesn't matter. We have to get the ring back." Rosa took her friend's hand and looked into her brown eyes. "We can do this, Nutmeg. We've stopped King Rat before and we can do it again. I know we can!"

Nutmeg took a deep breath. "OK, then, let's go!"

Nutmeg used her magic to take her and Rosa to the woods outside King Rat's castle. King Rat's magic was very powerful and he had placed enchantments on his castle grounds so that no one else could use strong magic there.

Rosa peered through the trees at the foreboding castle. King Rat had an army of human-sized mice who worked for him. They had pointed teeth and sharp swords.

"I can't see anyone—" She broke off as suddenly, the castle doors opened and the mouse guards came out. But they didn't look frightening at all. They came skipping out like school children – some were throwing balls at each other, others started to play hopscotch, three of them sat down to play a game of marbles, while another group played with some shiny trains and one played with a baby doll.

Rosa and Nutmeg exchanged astonished looks.

"What's going on?" whispered Nutmeg.

"They must have been caught up in the magical mix-up too," said Rosa.

"Of course! They're acting as if they're the children in *The Nutcracker*!" said Nutmeg.

Suddenly there was a loud burst of music. The door flew open and two figures came dancing out of the castle. One was the Nutcracker Soldier, dressed in his red and gold finery and the other…

Rosa stared at the person being twirled round and round, his expression outraged.

It was King Rat!

The Thief

The Nutcracker Soldier swung round in a
joyful dance. King Rat's crown was now
slipping to the side of his head and his
cloak was hanging off one shoulder. "Get
off me! GET OFF!" he was shouting, trying
to pull himself free. But the Nutcracker
simply twirled him faster across the grass.

Rosa started to giggle. "It looks like King

Rat's been caught in the mix-up too!"

The Nutcracker let go of King Rat and leaped dramatically into the air with a *grand jeté* before dancing away.

King Rat shook his fist at him. Then he straightened his crown and looked round at his usually fierce mice. Seeing them all

playing games, he buried his head in his
paws.

"It doesn't look like he's having much
fun," Rosa whispered quickly to Nutmeg.
"Maybe he'll decide he wants to give the
ring back."

"But how do we find out?" the fairy
asked.

Rosa hesitated and then made a brave
decision. She walked out of the trees!

She heard Nutmeg gasp. "What are you
doing?"

Rosa ignored her.

King Rat saw Rosa and pointed in
astonishment. "It's you! The dratted girl
with the ballet shoes! And you've got that
annoying fairy with you," he said as

Nutmeg ran to join Rosa. "How dare you both come to my castle uninvited!"

"I hope you've got a plan, Rosa!" Nutmeg whispered in a quavering voice as King Rat strode towards them. His fur was a greasy black and he had a long pointed nose and red eyes.

"Guards, get them!" he yelled. But the guards were too busy playing with their toys.

Rosa's heart pounded in her chest as she stared bravely at the rodent. "We know you've got the King's ring and we want it back." She thought about the look of horror on King Rat's face as the Nutcracker had danced with him. "You don't want the ballets mixed up any more than anyone else does. Give us the ring and then when it's returned to the King, everything will be all right again."

King Rat glared back at her. "Idiot girl! If it was that simple, don't you think I'd have given it back already?" He shook his head. "I can't give it back. It's broken."

"Broken!" Nutmeg exclaimed in horror.

King Rat's shoulders slumped. "That's why everything has gone wrong. If I still had it and it was all in one piece everything would be fine. But it's smashed to smithereens."

"How?" demanded Rosa.

"I dropped it," admitted King Rat. "It broke and then from that moment on, everything started going wrong." He reached into the pocket of his cloak and took out a small bag before shaking out a gold ring. It had a sparkling white stone that had obviously been glued together. There was one piece missing. "I couldn't find the last fragment."

"This is awful!" said Nutmeg. "If the

stone is broken, everything's going to stay mixed up forever!"

"I know," agreed King Rat gloomily. "I wish I'd never taken it. I only wanted it because it was so bright and shiny. Now life in Enchantia is never going to be the same again."

"There's nothing we can do," said Nutmeg, starting to cry.

Rosa put her arm around her friend and gave her a hug. "We can't give up that easily. Maybe *we* can find the missing piece of the ring." She looked at King Rat. "Where did you drop it?"

"Over there," he said, pointing back to the steps by the front door.

"Well, let's get looking!" said Rosa.

Rosa, Nutmeg and King Rat hunted around. The mouse guards nearby were arguing. "You must have taken my train! It was here a minute ago," said one. "You just wanted it because it was so shiny!"

"I didn't take it! I didn't!" said the second mouse.

"Did too!" whinged the first.

"Did not!"

Rosa began to think she preferred the guards when they were scary!

"Oh, this is useless! We've looked everywhere," King Rat said grumpily after ten minutes. He sat down in the shade of a nearby tree with massive leaves and took off his shoes with a groan. "My feet are killing me from all the dancing that the Nutcracker keeps making me do. I'm going to have a rest." He leaned against the tree trunk and closed his eyes.

"Maybe we should just give up,"
Nutmeg said to Rosa.

"No! The missing bit of stone can't have
just disappeared," said Rosa as King Rat
started to snore loudly. "Let's keep looking."

Nutmeg laid her wand down on the
ground and crouched on her hands and knees,
examining every inch of the grass. Rosa
joined in too, but no matter how much they
hunted, they couldn't find the missing piece.

Nutmeg sighed. "It's no use, Rosa," she said, getting to her feet at last. "We're not going to find it. We—" she broke off. "Where's my wand? I left it here!" She pointed at the ground. "It's gone!"

"It can't have gone," said Rosa.

Nutmeg turned on King Rat, who was just waking up. "Have you taken my wand?" she demanded.

"What would I want with your stupid sparkly wand!" snorted King Rat. He got to his feet and reached for his boots. He gave a yell. "Hey! Someone's stolen the buckle off my boot!" He swung round to Nutmeg. "Give it back!"

"It wasn't me. I haven't touched your smelly boot!" said Nutmeg. "You're just saying that because you took my wand."

"I didn't take it!"

"You must have!"

"Stop it, both of you!" Rosa broke in. "Nutmeg hasn't taken the buckle off your boot," she said to King Rat. "She's been with me, looking for the missing piece of the moonstone all the time you've been

asleep. And King Rat can't have taken your wand," she said to the fairy. "He's been snoring away like anything."

"I do not snore!" said King Rat indignantly.

Rosa ignored him. "There has to be another explanation."

Just then there was a shout from the guards and a flash of black and white as a bird swooped across the courtyard and flew up into the tree with the big green leaves.

"My marble! My best shiny marble! That bird took it!" shouted one of the mice.

Of course! *A magpie!*

Rosa grinned at Nutmeg and King Rat.
"You know, I think we might just have
found the thief!"

Stolen Goods!

"Magpies often steal shiny things," Rosa explained to King Rat and Nutmeg. She looked up into the branches of the tree with the big leaves. "I bet he's got a nest in that tree. If we could get up to it, we'd probably find your wand and the buckle and all kinds of other things."

Nutmeg turned to King Rat. "If you lift

that spell of yours that stops me using
magic, I could fly up there and see," she
said, fluttering her wings.

King Rat hesitated.

"You want your buckle back, don't you?"
Rosa said to him.

"Oh, all right. What harm can it do?"
King Rat held up his paws and muttered a
spell under his breath.

Nutmeg spun round and rose into the air.
She flew up into the tree. The magpie
squawked from one of the branches.

"There is a nest up here but these leaves
are so big I can hardly see it!" Nutmeg
called down to Rosa and King Rat. She had
to pull a few of the leaves off to get to the
nest. They floated down to the ground.

"Can you see anything yet?" called Rosa.

"Yes! Here's my wand, and King Rat's buckle, marbles and a train and—" Nutmeg broke off with a gasp. "Oh, goodness! Wait until you see this!"

She flew down and landed lightly on her pointes, her arms full of the things she had found. She quickly handed back the buckle, the train and the marble, slipped her wand into a pocket in her tutu and then held out her hand. "Look!" Slowly, she opened her fingers.

Rosa held her breath. *Could it be… was it really…?* "It's the missing piece of moonstone!" she gasped.

Nutmeg beamed. "The magpie must have taken it as well!"

"Where's the ring?" Rosa quickly asked King Rat.

"Here." He held it out.

Rosa took it and quickly added the

missing piece. It fitted
perfectly! The ring
was complete
again.

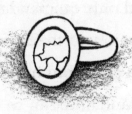

She glanced round, expecting something
to happen – some music or some magic. But
everything stayed exactly the same. The
guards kept playing as if they were
children.

"Maybe we need some glue!" King Rat
hurried inside and came back with a tube.
He carefully stuck the piece of stone into
the ring, but *still* nothing happened.

"Why's it not working?" said Rosa.

Nutmeg bit her lip. "I think I might
know. I remember when I was little, people
said that if the ring was ever broken it

could only be mended by the First Fairy
coming back to Enchantia. I thought it was
just a story, but maybe it is real."

"Well, how can we get her to come here?"
Rosa asked.

"The only way to do it is to get at least
one person from every ballet to join in a
dance," Nutmeg answered.

"We can't do that," said King Rat. "There
are too many ballets."

Even Rosa felt stumped. How could they
possibly get one person from every ballet
together? "Oh," she said, her heart sinking.
"That's going to be impossible, isn't it?
We'd have to travel round for days and
days."

"Hang on!" Nutmeg said, suddenly

seizing her hands, her eyes shining. "It's not impossible at all! In Enchantia we can summon anyone by doing a bit of their dance from the ballet they come from."

Rosa stared. "Really?"

"Yes! So I could dance and summon some people and then they could dance too and help us summon more people." Nutmeg twirled round in excitement.

"Soon we'd have everyone we need!"

"But… but that means there would be lots of people dancing!" King Rat exclaimed. "Here! Outside my castle!"

Nutmeg nodded.

"NO!" yelled King Rat, burying his head in his hands. "I'll never live this down!"

Ignoring King Rat, Rosa and Nutmeg hurried away. "I'll do the dancing to summon the first few people and as they arrive, you can explain what's happening and get them to dance too," said Nutmeg.

She waved her wand. Music flowed through the air. Rosa recognised it immediately. It was the Sugar Plum Fairy's

music from *The Nutcracker*. Nutmeg began
to dance. Rosa couldn't help herself, she
had to join in. She couldn't go up on her
pointes like Nutmeg but she moved
lightly across the grass, copying as best
she could. Nutmeg caught her eyes and
grinned at her.

A minute later there was a lilac flash, and
Nutmeg's sister, the beautiful Sugar Plum
Fairy, appeared. She was wearing a lilac
tutu and had a sparkling tiara in her hair.

"Oh, not her too!" King Rat groaned from
the castle.

"What's going on?" Sugar asked.

"Rosa will explain!" called Nutmeg,
waving her wand again. The music
changed to a sweet melody, full of longing.
Nutmeg began to dance round, as if she
was holding a broom in her hands.

"Cinderella's music!" cried Rosa. She
turned to Sugar. "We're trying to summon a
character from every single ballet," she
explained. "So that we can do a dance to
make the First Fairy appear!" Quickly she

told Sugar everything that had happened.

"I'll help!" Sugar said eagerly. She waved her own wand and began to do a dance that Rosa recognised as part of the swans' dance from *Swan Lake*. After a few minutes, three great white swans came flapping across the sky.

By now Cinderella had appeared and she had started to do the Lilac Fairy's dance from *Sleeping Beauty* and Nutmeg was dancing a new dance that Rosa had never seen before. Suddenly a rosy-cheeked girl in a bright costume appeared.

"Swanhilda from the ballet *Coppelia*," Sugar cried to Rosa as she twirled past, jumping into the air and summoning the Prince from *The Firebird*. "It's working, Rosa! It's really working! Everyone's coming!"

The First Fairy

Rosa's head spun with all the different music. Within minutes the area outside the castle had filled with people. They were all shouting out, asking what was going on. Rosa couldn't get round them all fast enough to explain.

"We've done it!" Sugar exclaimed. "We've got someone from every ballet!"

"Although half of them don't know why they're here yet," said Nutmeg, looking worried. "How are we going to tell them they all have to do a dance? They're being so noisy!"

"What we need is a megaphone, or something that would work as one!" said Rosa. What could they do? Her eyes fell on the enormous leaves that had fallen from the tree and an idea came to her. Hurrying over to one, she rolled it up into a cone-like shape.

She ran up the steps and shouted through it. "Quiet, please! QUIET!"

Gradually the noise died down. Rosa blushed as everyone turned to look at her. "I know some of you are wondering why

72

you're here," she said. "Well, the thing is, we need everyone's help to get all the ballets back to normal. The King's moonstone ring is broken and to mend it we need to summon the First Fairy." A buzz of excited chatter rose. She raised her voice again. "We need you all to do a dance and..." She broke off as she realised she didn't know what the dance was!

Sugar saw Rosa's confusion and jumped up beside her, taking the megaphone. "I can show you what to do, everyone. It's very simple. The important thing is that you all

do it at the same time in a circle, and we
keep doing it until the First Fairy appears."

She used her wand to make a lively tune
play and then she ran down the steps and
began to dance – three steps to the right,
followed by a turn, another three steps,
followed by another turn. "Copy me!" she
called. "This is all you have to do!"

Everyone began to join in.

"Come on!" Nutmeg said, pulling Rosa
into the dance.

Rosa's heart soared. She hadn't been
sure if she would be included, not being a
character from a ballet, but there was
nothing she wanted more than to dance to
the music. Dancing joyfully with the
others in the circle, she lost herself in the

music, stepping
and turning,
stepping and
turning until her head
whirled.

*I wish the examiners
could see me now*, she
thought.

A new piece of
music broke in on
top of the first. It was different, slow and
gentle, piercingly sweet. It swelled in
loudness, gradually getting stronger. It gave
Rosa the feeling of dawn breaking in the
morning. The lively music faded
underneath it and gradually everyone
slowed down and stopped.

"Look!" Rosa breathed. In the centre of the circle a golden haze was forming. A figure appeared in the middle of it and the mist cleared. A beautiful fairy, dressed all in gold with a tiara on her pale blonde hair, was standing in a perfect *arabesque*, balanced on one toe, her other leg held straight out behind her, her arms stretched out. She looked like a bird caught in mid-flight.

Rosa felt like she never wanted to take her eyes off her. The fairy's face was beautiful, calm and serene, and the air around her seemed to sparkle. Everyone watched in awe as she slowly brought her leg down until her feet were together and then she turned on her pointes and looked straight at Rosa.

Dancing quickly with a fast-turning step, the First Fairy spun out of the centre of the circle and stopped in front of Rosa. She held out her wand and looked invitingly at her. Rosa didn't need her to say anything. She knew what she had to do. She held the ring out in front of her.

The fairy gracefully touched the moonstone with her wand. There was a

 flash of golden light. Rosa looked at it and gasped. "It's mended!"

The music rose and swelled. The First Fairy smiled and then she spun away round the circle, dancing faster and faster. As the music reached the final note, she jumped into the air in a *grand jeté* and vanished, leaving just a faint gold mist shimmering behind her.

There was a moment's silence and then suddenly everyone started to talk at once.

"It was the First Fairy!"

"She was really here!"

"And she mended the ring!"

"Are the ballets all right now?"

Rosa looked around. King Rat's guards

were slowly standing up. They looked dazed and confused.

"Marbles!" said one.

"Hopscotch!" said another, looking at the marks on the floor.

"Playing with dolls!" said a third, hastily throwing down the baby doll he had been cuddling. He made a big effort to snarl and look vicious. "What's going on? I *hate* dolls unless I'm chewing on them to sharpen my teeth! Yuck!"

"You're back to normal!" King Rat shouted in delight. "Yahoo!"

"Everything's back to normal!" said Sugar in relief.

The crowd of people cheered.

"Oh, Rosa. Thank you for helping us!" said Nutmeg, hugging her friend.

Sugar smiled at her. "We'd never have solved the problem without you, Rosa."

"I was sure it was impossible," said Nutmeg.

Rosa grinned. "Nothing's impossible," she said.

"Well, apart from maybe making King Rat like dancing!" Nutmeg giggled.

"Hmm." A mischievous twinkle lit up Sugar's eyes and for a moment the two sisters looked very similar. Sugar glanced to where King Rat was marching around yelling at his guards. "King Rat hasn't put his enchantment back yet that stops anyone doing magic here, has he?"

Nutmeg shook her head.

"Then let me see what I can do!" Sugar waved her wand.

A lively polka swelled through the air.

"Oh, not MORE dancing!" King Rat said, looking around as people cheered again and started to grab partners. They began to take light galloping sideways steps, swinging each other round.

Sugar danced over, pointed her wand at King Rat's boots and quickly said a magic spell:

"*Boots twirl and spin, turn and prance,*

Make King Rat love to dance!"

"What? No!" King Rat yelled in horror as there was a lilac flash and suddenly his feet started to move of their own accord. But as he

began to spin
round, the horror
turned to surprise
and his mouth
turned upwards
in a grin.

"Actually,
this is quite
fun!" he
shouted. "I'm
dancing! Really dancing! Hey, wait
for me!" He galloped away with great
galumphing steps after the others, turning
round and round, his cloak flying out
behind him, his red eyes lit up with delight.

Rosa gasped. "So King Rat likes dancing
now!"

"Not forever, unfortunately. My magic's not strong enough for that. The spell will wear off after a bit." Sugar giggled. "But it will be fun watching him until it does!"

"Come on!" said Nutmeg, taking Rosa's hands. "Let's join in!"

They set off with Sugar dancing beside them. Rosa laughed in delight as they all swept around the castle in a laughing, happy throng. This was the best adventure ever! But then her feet started to tingle. Her ballet shoes were glowing.

"I'm about to go home!" she cried.

And in a whirl of sparkling colours, she felt herself being whisked away!

Nothing's Impossible

Rosa felt her feet hit the floor and the colours faded. She blinked. She was back in the exam room and Rebecca was dancing the set dance.

For a moment, Rosa felt dazed. So much had been happening in Enchantia that she had completely forgotten all about the exam. But now it came flooding back. *I've*

messed up, she realised as Olivia started her dance. *I'm never going to pass.*

She felt a wave of despair. She wanted to give up. *No*, she thought, remembering what had just happened in Enchantia. *Nothing's impossible.*

Rosa took a deep breath. Maybe it was too late and she had failed already, but she had to try. She still had her set dance and character work to do. Maybe if she gave it her very best shot she still had a chance to pass.

Olivia finished and suddenly it was Rosa's turn. She danced forward. Usually when she danced she talked herself through the steps in her head, but she knew the steps so well from all her practising that her body seemed to take over, and this time she just danced. She spun and jumped and ended perfectly, one arm high, the other by her side, her shoulders down, her chin lifted, her body poised and graceful.

As the music stopped she relaxed, a huge grin spreading over her face. She'd done it! Whether she passed or not she knew she had tried her very best and that was all that really mattered.

Quickly she joined the others. Now there was just the character dance to go!

"Oh, wow!" Olivia gasped as the door shut behind them after the exam had finished. "You were amazing, Rosa! I've never seen you dance so well. Your set dance and character dance were brilliant!"

"Thanks," Rosa said in relief. "I really messed up in the centre, though."

"Well, I got so much wrong at the *barre*," said Asha.

"And I forgot the steps in the character dance," groaned Rebecca.

"I certainly won't have passed. It's impossible," said Rosa.

"Nothing's impossible. You should know that by now, Rosa," Madame Za-Za said

briskly, opening the door of the changing rooms. "Come along, girls." She ushered them into the changing rooms. "Don't worry about what you got wrong; everyone makes mistakes in an exam. No one is ever perfect. I'm sure you all did your best and that is the most important thing."

Two weeks later, Rosa arrived at the ballet school with Olivia. They were greeted at the door by Asha. "The exam results are up!" she exclaimed. "Quick! Come and see!"

Rosa and Olivia both hurried down the corridor. A piece of white paper was pinned to the noticeboard outside Madame Za-Za's office.

Rosa's heart pounded. She had been trying not to think about the exam. She knew she must have failed after making so many mistakes early on. She reached the notice, but the words seemed to swirl in front of her eyes as she tried to find her name.

Please let me have passed, please let me have passed, she prayed.

Olivia gave a massive squeal. "We both passed!" she said. "We did it! Look!" She pointed her finger at the paper and Rosa saw the words:

Olivia Rowley… A (distinction)

Rosa Maitland… A (distinction)

She had passed! And with distinction! She could hardly believe it.

She hugged Olivia. "Oh, wow! Oh, wow! Oh, wow!"

Madame Za-Za came out of her office and smiled at them. "Well done, girls. I'm very proud of you both."

"Thank you, Madame Za-Za!" Olivia gasped.

Madame Za-Za's eyes met Rosa's. "You see. As long as you never give up, nothing is impossible, Rosa," she said softly.

And in that moment, Rosa knew that she was right.

Darcey's Magical Masterclass

The Spell of the First Fairy

The First Fairy saved Enchantia with her spell to fix the moonstone. In the steps below try imaging that you are holding her wand as you move your arm around in graceful sweeping movements.

1.
Place your feet in 1st position, with your ankles together and toes pointing outwards. Rest your left arm on the barre and hold your right arm out to the side.

2.
Stretch over to the side, sweeping your arm over your head; keep your arm in a lovely oval shape.

3.
Rise back up, bringing your arm in front of you before sweeping it back out to the side.

4.
Swoosh your arm round in a circle in front of you until it is back to the side again. Start again and keep going until your magic is done!

PS (If you don't have an actual barre you could rest your hand on a wall or fence instead… remember to swap over so you can try the magic with your other arm!)

Magic Ballerina™
Rosa and the Special Prize

The ruler of the underwater kingdom has accused
King Tristan of taking his special sceptre and has cast
a storm spell over Enchantia until it's returned! Will
Rosa be able to find out who really has the sceptre?

Read on for a sneak preview
of Rosa and the Special Prize...

∘⊙.*.☆.⊙.*.☆.⊙.*.☆.⊙.*.∘

The silvery light cleared and Rosa saw that she was by the sea. The waves were stormy and grey and a cold wind was whipping through her hair. Rosa shivered and looked around. She'd never been in this part of Enchantia before. Why had the magic brought her here?

"Rosa!"

Rosa looked around to see Nutmeg, the fairy of the spices, standing at the top of the cliff, being blown about by the gusts of wind.

"Hi, Nutmeg!" Rosa called.

Nutmeg came scrambling down the cliff. She reached the bottom and ran over. She hugged Rosa. "I'm very glad you've come, Rosa."

"It's freezing here!" said Rosa, hugging her back.

Nutmeg nodded. "There's stormy weather all the time at the moment – because King Tristan has fallen out with King Neptune... A few days ago, Neptune's special sceptre was stolen; he was so angry that he sent storms all over the land. Everyone is really miserable because it's too windy to dance outside, and the thunder drowns out any music inside so we can't dance anywhere!"

"Well, why doesn't King Tristan just give it back?" asked Rosa.

"Because he hasn't got it," said Nutmeg. "He didn't take it. He's got absolutely no idea where it is. The only way to stop the storms is to find the sceptre and give it back. Everyone's been looking and no one has found it yet. I just don't know what we're going to do..."

°｡⁺ ☆ ｡⁺ ☆ ｡⁺ ☆ ｡⁺ °

Magic Ballerina

Holly and the Dancing Cat

Darcey Bussell

*To Phoebe and Zoe, as they are the inspiration
behind Magic Ballerina.*

Contents

Prologue

*In the soft, pale light, the girl stood
with her head bent and her hands
held lightly in front of her.
There was a moment's silence and then
the first notes of the music began.
For as long as the girl could remember
music had seemed to tell her of
another world – a magical, exciting
world – that lay far, far away.
She always felt if she could just
close her eyes and lose herself,
then she would get there.
Maybe this time. As the music
swirled inside her, she swept
her arms above her head, rose on to
her toes and began to dance…*

1

Holly

Holly Wilde swept her arms in a circle and danced forward with slow steps to the haunting, beautiful music. She stopped on her right leg, one arm above her head, the other out to the side. She paused, before gracefully bringing her arm down and moving around her bedroom, turning slowly again and again, lost in her dance.

Holly loved the ballet of *Sleeping Beauty*.
Most people remembered the *Rose Adagio*,
the famous dance that the princess did before
she pricked her finger, but Holly had always
preferred the piece of music she was dancing
to now, where Sleeping Beauty appeared to
the prince in a magic vision. It had a lilting,
slightly ghostly melody. Sweeping her arms
upwards, she pirouetted around as the music
came to an end. She stopped, trembling with
the joy of dancing. Closing her eyes, she
imagined that she had just danced off stage
and that the audience were clapping wildly.

Just like they did when Mum danced it in
New York...

Sinking down on to her bed, Holly glanced
at the photoframe on the chest of drawers of

her mum, Bella. Her eyes, the same mossy-green as Holly's, were shining. Her dark hair was caught up in a diamond tiara.

Holly picked the picture up, her own straight dark hair falling forward across her face. Her heart ached. *Oh Mum*, she thought, for about the thousandth time, *why did you have to leave me here? Why couldn't I have stayed with you?*

She remembered the day she had come to live at Aunt Maria's and Uncle Ted's, back in

July. She heard her mum's words as she had left: "I'll miss you so much, darling. But you're ten now and you can't keep on travelling around with me, you need to stay in one place, go to one school and make friends. Aunt Maria and Uncle Ted will look after you and in the holidays you can come and join me or your dad just as you always have."

"But I don't want to stay here," Holly had protested.

"I know," her mum had said softly, tears in her eyes. "But you have to. We'll see each other soon."

She had kissed Holly and then she had

gone. She had phoned and emailed lots, but she was touring America and it was so far away that Holly hadn't been able to visit her. She had seen her dad for a few weeks in August when he had been performing in London. He was a dancer too, but he and her mum had got divorced six years ago, so she only ever saw him separately.

And now here she was. Midway through a new term and taking ballet classes after school. She'd started at Madame Za-Za's just before the summer holidays, but she hadn't really made much of an effort to make friends with any of the other girls. She had just felt too unhappy and, anyway, with all the moving round she'd done in her life, she'd learned it was better not to make friends. You only ended up having to say goodbye. And so she'd kept herself pretty much to herself in Madame Za-Za's class, concentrating on her ballet and coldly brushing off all the other girls' offers of friendship. To her relief, they had quickly decided to leave her alone.

Well, all apart from one…

Rosa Maitland had been really friendly. She'd left to go to the Royal Ballet School in London, but before she'd gone, she had given Holly a pair of old red ballet shoes. Holly kept them on a shelf above her desk. The words Rosa had said as she had pushed them into Holly's hands echoed through her head: "I hope you find out how special they are."

Holly frowned and, getting up, went over to them. They were old and the leather was very soft, but there didn't seem to be anything that special about them as far as she could see. Picking them up, she felt a tingle, like the faintest electric shock. Maybe she'd try them on again anyway…

"Holly! Time to go to ballet!" Aunt Maria's voice called up the stairs.

Holly put the shoes down on her desk and hurried out of the room.

Head up, shoulders down, extend the arms, remember to smile…

Holly and the other girls in her class at
Madame Za-Za's ballet school went through
the familiar sequence of exercises, first at the
barre and then in the centre of the room.

Holly worked hard. Madame Za-Za was a
very elegant woman with greying-brown
hair held up in loose bun and lots of bangles.
Holly knew Madame Za-Za had been a
prima ballerina when she was younger. Her
mum had said what an amazing teacher she

was, but although Holly worked hard, she longed to be back with her mum, learning from her instead.

"Into pairs," Madame Za-Za called as she turned to change the music on the CD player.

There was usually an even number of girls in the class so someone always had to go with Holly, but that day one of the girls was away and she was left on her own, the other girls pairing up quickly. Eventually there were just two of the newer girls left, Chloe and Alyssia. They raced past where Holly was standing in the middle to take each other's hands. As they met up, they smiled in relief.

Holly felt a pang. She didn't want to make friends, but it was hard to be left out quite so obviously. Chloe happened to glance at her and looked suddenly guilty. "Holly, you could come with us… make a three," she called impulsively.

Holly heard the horror in Alyssia's hiss. "Chloe!"

"No thanks," said Holly, folding her arms and turning away.

Just then, Madame Za-Za looked round. "Ah, Holly, you haven't got a partner. Why don't you…"

"I'll dance on my own," Holly interrupted. No one ever interrupted Madame Za-Za, who was quite strict, but Holly couldn't bear the thought of being made to join a pair and watch the other two girls exchange looks. She knew she sounded haughty, but she didn't care.

Madame Za-Za raised an eyebrow. "Very well," she said, her eyes sweeping back to the other girls. "Now everyone, I'd like you to listen to this piece of music and imagine you are two leaves on the branch of a tree in autumn, fluttering in the breeze, about to fall…"

Holly danced on her own. *I don't care. I don't care.* She kept repeating the words in her head as she let the music flow over her, taking her away and making her feel like she was falling on the breeze, turning around, using her

115

movements to express the feelings of wistfulness and sadness inside her.

I don't want to be friends with any of them anyway. I don't need them, she thought and then she lost herself in the music and thought no more.

"Very good expressive work, Holly," Madame Za-Za praised at the end.

Holly gave her a small, tight smile. Now that the dancing was over she wanted to get out of there as quickly as possible. As soon as Madame Za-Za dismissed them, Holly hurried away.

I'll put Sleeping Beauty *on again*, she told herself as she changed out of her ballet shoes. Her muscles were aching from hard work, but she knew the one thing that would make her feel better was dancing.

Cramming her stuff into her bag, she left the changing rooms.

"Holly, wait!" she heard a voice call as she half-ran down the corridor.

She turned round and saw Chloe, coming out of the changing rooms. "I'm sorry you had to dance on your own today," she said. She hesitated. "Um, you could always come round to mine sometime. I don't know many people here, either."

Holly was sure she saw pity in Chloe's blue eyes. Unhappiness swept through her. How dare Chloe pity her! She'd travelled all over the world and met more ballet dancers than Chloe could even dream of.

"Why don't you ask your mum if you can come round for tea next week?" Chloe suggested.

Holly's temper exploded. "I'm hardly likely to ask my mum when she's in America, am I? Anyway, I don't want to be friends with you or with anyone here. Just leave me alone!"

And, swinging round, Holly stormed out of the front door.

The Dancing Cat

Holly ran down the drive of the ballet school, her feet slipping slightly on the fallen leaves. It was October now and the sun was low in the sky.

Her Uncle Ted was waiting in the car outside. "How was class?"

"Fine," Holly muttered, shutting the door hard.

But as they drove home, Holly's temper faded and Chloe's hurt face refused to leave her mind. She started to feel guilty. Chloe hadn't known about her mum being away. She had only been trying to be nice.

When they reached the house she went straight up to her bedroom. It had been a horrible afternoon. All she wanted to do was dance and block everything out.

As she put her ballet bag down on her desk, the back of her hand touched the red ballet shoes. She felt the familiar spark tingle her fingers and picked them up. She would wear them. Shrugging off her hooded top, she quickly pulled them on and put on the same music as before.

Holly moved forward with slow graceful

steps and as she danced,
everything else
faded away. But
then, moving into an
arabesque, she became
aware that her feet were
tingling.

She looked down and
gasped in astonishment. The
red ballet shoes were
glowing and sparkling!

"Oh!" she exclaimed. Bright colours
surrounded her and the next second she felt
herself being lifted into the air and whisked
away!

Holly came to rest on a bed of fallen leaves. The bright colours faded and she looked around, her heart thudding. She was standing in the middle of a wood! Red, gold and brown leaves were lying thickly on the ground. A squirrel scampered up a nearby tree, pausing to give her a curious look.

Holly's mind was spinning. What had happened?

It didn't feel anything like a dream. She could hear birds chirruping, smell the damp woods. She bent down and touched the leaves on the ground. They were cool beneath her fingers…

"Oh, my shimmering whiskers! It's you! The girl with the red shoes!"

Holly looked up and promptly fell over in

shock as a huge white cat came dancing towards her. He was on two legs and slightly taller than her and he was wearing white ballet shoes, a black hat with a feather in and a gold waistcoat. He leaped through the air,

one leg stretched behind and one in front, in a perfect *grand jeté*. Landing beside her, he pirouetted around, before grabbing both of her hands.

"This is so brilliant!" he cried, looking

completely delighted as he pulled her to her feet. Up close, she saw his eyes were a beautiful deep emerald green and his silvery whiskers sprang out at the side of his face. "We knew the shoes had a new owner and we have all been wondering when we would get to meet you. And now I have! Oh, how lucky I am! What's your name?"

"Holly," she answered automatically.

The cat bowed. "And I am the White Cat."

He jumped into the air, spinning round in excitement. "It's amazing to meet you, Holly."

"Where… where am I?" Holly stammered.

"In Enchantia, the land where all the characters from the ballets live," the cat replied. His fluffy tail flicked over his shoulder and he pointed at her feet. "The ballet shoes you're wearing were created with some of the strongest magic in Enchantia. Whenever we are in trouble, they bring their owner – a human girl – here to help fix things. Someone from Enchantia gets to meet them first and be their friend, and this time it looks like it's me!"

Holly stared at him. Was she really in a strange magic land full of people like talking cats who came from the different ballets? Had she been sent there to help them solve their problems? Although she had to admit it sounded very exciting, an image of Chloe came into her head followed by a picture of her mum waving goodbye.

"Look, I'm sorry, I've enough problems of my own right now," she said quickly. "I just can't fix other people's problems too. Maybe another time." She turned away, wondering how she got the shoes to take her home. She tried wishing.

I wish I could go back, she thought. But nothing happened.

Remembering *The Wizard of Oz*, she clicked her heels together three times. Still nothing happened.

The White Cat walked curiously round her. "What are you doing?"

Holly turned away. She didn't want to see him; she wanted to get back to her bedroom. *Think carefully*, she told herself. She'd been dancing when the shoes had worked before, so maybe that was what she had to do?

She ran forward and turned a pirouette. *Home, home, home*, she thought as hard as she could, shutting her eyes. But when she blinked them open again she was still standing in the wood.

The White Cat leapt joyously in front of her. "Oh, is this a game, Holly? I like games!

Look how many pirouettes I can do!" He
turned round on the spot so many times that
Holly's mouth dropped open.

"It's not a game. I just want to go home!"
she exclaimed. "I have to. For a start, my
aunt and uncle are going to be really worried
about me..."

"No, they won't be," interrupted the cat.
"No time will pass in the human world
while you are here. You'll go back and it will
be as if you haven't been away."

"But I can't stay," Holly protested. "Look,
will you please just tell me how I get these
shoes to work and take me home?"

"You can't make the shoes do what you
want." The White Cat's brilliant eyes met
hers. "They'll take you back when the

problem is solved, but you won't be able to make them take you back before. The magic doesn't work like that."

"Oh." Holly sat down on a fallen tree trunk. "So I'm really stuck here?" she said faintly.

"It's not that bad, is it?" the White Cat said, giving her a hopeful look.

Holly felt tears prickle her eyes. She dashed them away with the back of her hand.

"Oh, I see." The cat looked suddenly

deflated, like an old balloon. "It really is that bad." He sat down on the log and shook his head. "I don't understand it. I've never heard of a human girl not wanting to help before." He twisted his tail anxiously in his paws. "It must be me. I must have messed things up. I was just so excited to meet you."

His pointed ears flattened unhappily.

Holly began to feel bad. "It's not your fault," she said.

"But it must be," the cat muttered sadly.

"It isn't."

Holly looked at his drooping ears. She couldn't bear it. "OK. Look, I will stay and help you."

The change was instant. The cat leaped up from the tree trunk, his ears back in points.

"Oh, my shimmering whiskers and glittering tail!" He jumped high into the air, crossing his feet over and over again. "That's wonderful! Thank you! Thank you, so much!" He grabbed her hands and twirled her around as fast as he could.

Despite her reluctance, Holly unexpectedly found herself starting to smile. His excitement was infectious. "So what do you need help with?" she gasped as they stopped and the world spun dizzily around her.

The White Cat smiled at her. "Sit down and I'll explain…"

Making Friends

"It all started this morning," the White Cat began to tell Holly. "It's exactly a year to the day since Princess Aurelia and Prince Florimund got married. The King and Queen are having a party this evening and the King has said that everyone who was at the wedding has to be there tonight to do the same dance that they did at the ceremony.

"I've been put in charge of organising it.
All the others arrived yesterday: the princes's
brother and two sisters; Princess Aurelia's
fairy godmother, Lila; the other fairies who
were at Aurelia's christening; Puss in Boots,
Goldilocks, Bluebeard and his wife, Little
Red Riding Hood, the bluebird, the
enchanted princess and all the palace
courtiers as well. We started practising the
dance, but then suddenly, just a few hours
ago, Red Riding Hood decided to go home."

"She just left?"

Holly still wasn't sure about being in this
land, but she could feel herself being drawn
more and more into the story she was hearing.

The White Cat nodded. "All of a sudden. I
found a note from her saying she'd decided

to go home. The trouble is that means we are now one person short for the dance. I was just on my way to her house to try and persuade her to come back, but now the shoes have solved the problem. You can take Red Riding Hood's place!"

Holly felt a rush of excitement. So to help him, all she had to do was dance with the characters from her favourite ballet? That sounded OK to her!

"I can't wait to get back to the palace and introduce you to everyone," continued the White Cat. "But I think we'd better just stop by at Red Riding Hood's house on the way. I just want to check she's all right. It's not like her to let people down." He pointed through the trees. "Her house is just over there.

We could go by magic, but it won't take us long to walk and I love the woods in autumn. Oh, Holly!" He rubbed her cheek with the side of his head. "I'm really glad I was the one to meet you and that you are the new owner of the shoes!"

Holly stroked his fur. She was secretly beginning to feel quite glad she was the new owner of the shoes too!

They started walking along the path.

"So tell me about you," the White Cat said curiously.

"I live with my aunt and uncle. My mum
and dad are ballet dancers." Holly quickly
told the White Cat about her life.

"You must miss your mum a lot," said the
White Cat with concern.

Holly nodded.

"But I bet you have lots of friends," he
went on.

"Um, not really," Holly admitted
awkwardly.

"Why not?"

Holly shrugged.

The White Cat
spun away, jumped
into the air and
touched his toes,
before landing lightly.

"Well, you've got me now!" He grabbed her hands and waltzed her down the path. Holly giggled. She didn't think she ever wanted a friend other than her mum before, but the White Cat was so much fun.

"So, tell me something more about you," he said eagerly. "What do you like? What don't you like? What are you scared of?"

Holly blinked at all the questions. "Um, well, I like ballet. I don't like school. What am I scared of? Not much really." She thought for a moment. "I don't like heights, I guess."

"I don't like water," admitted the White Cat. "I'm so scared of it. My brother, Puss in Boots, calls me a scaredy cat!" He looked around. "I know, shall we play a game on the way? What do you play in your world?"

"Um… tag?" said Holly.

"OK, I'll be it!" said the cat. "I'll count to ten."

Holly darted away through the trees to the left and scrambled up a bank.

"Wait!" the White Cat called in alarm. "I meant down the path, Holly! Not that way!"

But it was too late. As Holly reached the top of the bank, she realised that on the other side the bank fell steeply down into a swiftly-flowing river. In her surprise, she lost her balance. Her arms flailed and the next minute, she was rolling down the hill straight towards the water!

Into the River

The cold water made Holly gasp as she
splashed into the river. She tried to tread
water, gulping a mouthful of air as the
current started to tow her along.

"Help!"

The White Cat had reached the top of the
bank. Holly could see he looked terrified, but
he didn't hesitate. He bounded down the

bank on all fours and launched himself into the water, swimming like a tiger. Grabbing hold of the back of her leotard in his mouth, he pulled her swiftly back.

"You saved me!" cried Holly as he dragged her out on to the bank.

"Oh, my glimmering whiskers!" he gasped. "I thought you were going to drown!"

"You were so brave." Holly put her arms round him in relief and hugged him hard. "Thank you!"

The cat licked her face with his rough tongue. "You're very wet. I hope Red Riding

Hood has some clothes you can borrow.
Come on!"

It only took them a few minutes to reach Red
Riding Hood's little wooden cottage, but
when they got there they found, to their
surprise, that it was all closed up.

"I wonder why she isn't here?" said the
White Cat looking puzzled.

"Maybe she called in on some friends on
the way back," Holly suggested. She was
very cold and had started to shiver.

The White Cat noticed. "I'll find her later.
Right now, we'd better get back to the Royal
Palace and get you some dry clothes. I'll take
us there by magic." He held his long tail in

his hand and
swished it around
in a circle on the
ground. Then he
pulled Holly into
the circle. "Get
ready!" he cried.
His whiskers twitched.

Silver sparkles flew off them and suddenly
they were whizzing away!

His magic set them down in a large walled
courtyard in front of a beautiful palace with
pointed turrets and pearly white walls.

"Welcome to the Royal Palace!" declared
the White Cat.

"Oh... wow!" Holly breathed, looking round.

There was a group of dancers talking near the front door, a band of musicians, and servants setting out tables in the afternoon sun.

"Wait here a minute." The cat bounded energetically into the palace and reappeared a few seconds later with a long velvet cloak. He wrapped it around Holly. "There, that should warm you up!"

"Thanks," she said gratefully, snuggling into it. She couldn't stop staring at the dancers across the courtyard. They were all characters she knew from the ballet of *Sleeping Beauty* – the fairies, the bluebird, Puss in Boots, Bluebeard and the enchanted

princess. A few of them had noticed her
arrival and were pointing.

One of the fairies ran over. She had dark
brown hair caught up in a diamond tiara, a
lilac tutu and glittering wings.

"Hi I'm Lila, the Lilac Fairy – Princess

Aurelia's fairy godmother. Are you the new
owner of the ballet shoes?" she asked.

Holly nodded. "I'm Holly."

"Oh, I'm so glad you're here." The fairy's
face was worried. She turned to the White
Cat. "We've got a real problem, Cat."

"I know, Lila," he said airily. "But don't worry. The shoes have solved it. Holly can dance Red Riding Hood's part."

Lila shook her head. "No. You don't understand." She lowered her voice. "Goldilocks has gone too!"

"What?"

"Sssh," Lila said hastily as several of the other dancers looked round at the cat's loud exclamation. "I've been keeping it secret. No one else knows yet, but I found a note five minutes ago saying she's gone home." She lowered her voice further. "I'm really worried. They can't both just have decided to go home. Oh, Cat. I think the Wicked Fairy might be to blame."

"The Wicked Fairy?" Holly joined in.

The White Cat looked horrified. "The Wicked Fairy is the one who tried to spoil Aurelia's sixteenth birthday, by making her prick her finger on a spinning wheel that would make her sleep for a hundred years," he explained.

Lila bit her lip. "Look, I think trouble is afoot here, but I need to ask the King something before I say any more. Wait here. I'll be back in a moment." She ran inside.

The White Cat frowned. "I wonder what she's going to ask the king. Hmm, I think I'm going to go in and find out. You stay here Holly, I'll be back very soon."

And leaving Holly in the courtyard, he hurried inside too.

Kidnapped!

The minutes ticked by. Holly watched the dancers starting to practise the dance that was performed at the end of the wedding in *Sleeping Beauty*. It was a lively dance with lots of skipping and galloping and turning round in pairs. As the music played, Holly could feel her feet itching to join in. She was sure she could do it…

She was just edging closer when Lila came hurrying out of the palace. "Where's the White Cat?"

"He went after you," replied Holly, surprised.

Lila looked alarmed. "I didn't see him. Oh, no! We have to find him!"

She ran inside the palace. Holly raced after her. "What's the rush? He said he'd come back."

But Lila was too busy calling for their missing friend. "White Cat! Where are you?"

Holly spotted a piece of paper on the floor. "What's that?" She picked it up.

I've gone home. Tell them to cancel the dance. From the White Cat.

°ⓖ·*·☆·ⓖ·*·☆·ⓖ·*·☆·ⓖ·*·°

"Look!" Holly gasped. "But the White Cat wouldn't just leave!"

"Of course he wouldn't," said Lila. "Oh, Holly, this is dreadful. I think the Wicked Fairy has kidnapped him – along with Goldilocks and Red Riding Hood."

Holly's stomach felt as if it was full of icy water. "Why? Because she wants to ruin the party?"

Lila nodded. "Look, I'm going to tell you a secret," she said in a whisper. "I told King Tristan about it a while ago. He asked me not to tell anyone else, in case people got worried. However, when I asked him just now he said I could tell you and the White

Cat. He's hoping you can help. You see, the Wicked Fairy has a very good reason for wanting to stop the dance from happening."

Holly's heart was pounding. "What is it?"

"Well, you know the prince broke the Wicked Fairy's curse when he woke Aurelia by kissing her?" Lila asked.

Holly nodded.

"The truth is he only half broke it," Lila sighed. "Being Aurelia's special fairy godmother, I knew that the wedding dance had to be repeated at sunset today, exactly a year on from the wedding. If it isn't, then the Wicked Fairy's curse would fall again and everyone would go back to sleep. And this time there would be no one to save us. We wouldn't ever wake up."

Holly stared at Lila. "But that's awful!"

Lila nodded. "I'm sure the Wicked Fairy thinks that if enough people disappear, then everyone else will realise that she's up to something, panic and leave before sunset."

"So the dance won't happen and then her curse will fall," said Holly. "Oh, goodness." A thought crossed her mind. "But how can you be sure it is her?"

"When I was with the king we used my magic to look at her castle. We saw Red

Riding Hood and Goldilocks trapped in the tallest tower. It won't be long before the White Cat's taken there too." Tears filled Lila's eyes. "Oh, Holly, I don't know what to do!"

Holly's mind whirled. A picture of the White Cat filled her head. She remembered the fear on his face before he bounded into the river to save her. Now she had to be as brave and save him – and the others.

"We have to go to the Wicked Fairy's castle and rescue them, before anyone notices they have all gone," she declared. "How do we get there?"

"We can use my magic," said Lila, "but I don't know how we are going to get them out of the tower."

Holly thought for a moment. "Could we take a rope ladder?" she suggested.

"That's a brilliant idea!" exclaimed Lila. "There's a rope ladder in the store cupboard in the cellars." She ran off and came back a few minutes later with a coiled-up rope ladder. She took Holly's hands. "Are you ready?"

Holly nodded determinedly.

Lila waved her wand. "Then let's go!"

Rope Ladder Rescue

Lila's magic whisked them away in a cloud of purple sparkles and set them down behind a tree in the grounds of a forboding grey castle.

Holly peeped out. "Look, there's the White Cat!" she hissed, seeing her friend looking out of the tallest tower. "Oh, Lila let's go to the tower and then you can fly up there with one end of the ladder."

But just as she said this, the castle door
flew open. A big fairy dressed in tatty black
clothes stomped out. Holly and Lila quickly
shrank back behind the tree.

The Wicked Fairy had cruel dark eyes and
a long warty nose. Her grey hair was piled
on her head and there was a long black

wand in her hand with a crystal ball at the
top. Lizards dressed as footmen scampered
around her. She flicked her wand.
Immediately, there was a flash of green
smoke and a carriage appeared. Instead
of horses there were four more lizards
pulling it.

The Wicked Fairy cackled as she climbed
into it. "Take me to the Royal Palace!"
Picking up the reins, she lashed them
down on the lizards' backs. "Onwards,
you fools!"

The other lizards fearfully leapt up
behind her and the carriage set off down
the drive.

"Come on!" Holly said as soon as it had
disappeared from sight. She raced to the
tower with Lila flying overhead.

"Oh, my shimmering whiskers!" The
White Cat called down from the window.
"It's Holly and Lila!" Two girls joined him,
one in a red cloak, the other with long blonde
ringlets.

"We've got a rope ladder," Holly called.

She saw a strange
look flicker across
the cat's face.

"Oh, but…" his
voice trailed off.

"What?"

The cat hesitated
and then shook his
head. "Nothing."

Lila flew up to the
window and passed
one end inside.
"Quick!" As soon as
it was secure, she
flew down with the
other end. Holly
held it steady.

159

The White Cat helped Red Riding Hood over the sill and out of the window. She climbed nimbly down. "Thank you!" she gasped, jumping the last few metres.

Goldilocks came next. "We're free!" she said her blue eyes shining. "Thank you!"

"Come on!" Holly urged the White Cat.

He started to climb over the windowsill and then he hesitated.

"What's the matter?" she called as he climbed back inside.

"I… I can't do it. I didn't tell you, but I'm not just scared of water. I'm scared of heights as well! You'll have to go on without me."

Holly looked at him in dismay. "But what about when the Wicked Fairy comes back?"

"Don't worry about me," he said bravely.

"You have to get back before people realise we're all missing. Go!"

Holly shook her head. "No way! I'm not leaving you." She swallowed hard and then did the only thing she could think of – she started to climb the rope.

"Holly, stop it!" he shouted anxiously. "You're scared of heights too!"

Holly ignored him. Gritting her teeth, she climbed higher and higher. Not daring to look down she stared at his shocked face. Her heart was pounding and her legs were shaking, but she had to get him down from there. "If I can do it, so you can you," she gasped as she got near to the window.

But just as she spoke, her foot slipped.
With a cry of alarm she grabbed hold of the
rung she was on with both hands. Her legs
dangled free. With one bound the White Cat
was out of the
window and
racing down the
rope ladder towards
her head and arms first.
At the same time, Lila shot
into the air.

The White Cat reached
Holly first. He held her
hands on to the
ladder as she
found the lower
rung with her feet.

"Thank you!' she said weakly, gazing into his green eyes.

Lila appeared beside her. "Come back down. I'll go behind you. If you slip again, I'll catch you."

Holly slowly backed down the rope ladder, Lila behind and the White Cat above. When they all reached the bottom she sank on to the ground, her legs too shaky to hold her up. The White Cat collapsed beside her and she stroked his soft fur.

His eyes blinked up at her. "You know for someone who says they don't have any friends, you're very good at being one, Holly."

Holly blushed.

Lila danced forward. "I'm just glad you're both safe."

"It was so scary," said Goldilocks.

"Thank you so much for rescuing us," said Red Riding Hood.

"We'd better get back," said Lila. "I just hope the others haven't realised we've all gone. You three go with the White Cat. I'll fly up and untie the ladder and follow with my own magic."

The White Cat helped Holly up as Lila
flew to the top of the ladder, but just then a
loud shriek tore through the air over the
sound of carriage wheels.

Holly gasped. The Wicked Fairy was
coming down the drive!

"No!" the fairy shrieked, her wand raised
and pointing straight at them!

A Tangly Solution

Holly and the others froze in fear. The Wicked
Fairy yanked the lizards to a stop and jumped
out. "I saw you in my crystal ball!" she cried,
her black eyes burning as she brandished her
wand. "I saw you trying to escape. Well, you
won't!" She pointed the wand at them again.
"With this wand's strongest power, I banish
you all to my highest…"

She broke off as the end of a rope ladder came flying down from the sky and conked her on the head. "OW!" she shrieked.

"Lila!" gasped Holly, looking up.

"What's happening?" hissed the Wicked Fairy, as Lila started flying in rapid circles, winding the rope ladder around the fairy. She flailed her arms and they got caught in the rope. "Help me, you fools!" she shrieked at her servants. But the lizards just stood there.

"Let's see how you like being imprisoned!" Lila flew around her legs at lightning speed.

The Wicked Fairy screeched and fell over on her back. The rope ladder was wrapped around her like a cocoon. She looked like a giant beetle struggling on the ground!

"Oh well done, Lila!" Holly cried. "That was brilliant!"

"Get me out of here!" yelled the Wicked Fairy to her servants as she rocked from side to side.

"Well, shimmering whiskers, it looks like no one is going to help you," said the White

Cat with a grin. "Maybe you should have said please!"

The Wicked Fairy shrieked in fury and drummed her feet on the ground.

Holly looked at the sky and realised that the sun was setting. The Wicked Fairy might be trapped, but the dance had to be performed or her curse would still work. "Come on everyone!" she cried. "Let's get back to the palace!"

The White Cat and Lila's magic whisked them away. A crowd of dancers rushed towards them as they landed in the courtyard.

"It's Red Riding Hood!"

"And Goldilocks!"

"Where have you all been? We were just getting worried about you!"

The hubbub of voices rose.

"We'll explain later!" the White Cat exclaimed. "But the sun is about to set and we have to do the dance now!"

Holly realised there was music playing and the tables around the courtyard had now been laid out with plates of food and massive jugs of fruit punch. A trumpeter rang out a loud fanfare.

"Quick! Into your positions!" cried the cat. "There's no time to waste."

Everyone dashed to stand around the courtyard, hands held elegantly, faces turned expectantly to the palace doors. The door

was opened by a page and the King and
Queen stepped through.

The crowd all bowed.

Holly joined in with the White Cat and
Lila. She didn't have a clue what she was
doing, but it was just so amazing to be here,
watching everything.

The King looked in their direction. Lila nodded at him as if to say it's all right. Holly saw him breathe a sigh of relief and his mouth moved in a silent thank you.

With a beaming smile, he led the Queen to where two golden thrones had been set. As they sat down there was another fanfare and Princess Aurelia and Prince Florimund appeared in the doorway.

Holly caught her breath. The princess had long dark wavy hair and big blue eyes. She was very beautiful. The music changed and the princess ran into the centre of the courtyard and turned a pirouette. With a leap, the prince was by her side. He took her hand and they began a graceful *pas de deux*. In the final moments, the princess turned

with incredible speed on her pointes, moving round the courtyard and finishing with a dramatic dive towards the floor. The prince caught her and then Aurelia danced away, beckoning everyone to join in. The music changed again becoming bold and lively.

They all formed a circle and began to dance
the graceful dance that Holly had seen them
practising earlier.

The White Cat pulled her into the dance
too. Holly eagerly joined in. With one hand
holding the White Cat's and the other
extended elegantly out to the side, she ran
and skipped, ran and
skipped. He
turned her
under his arm
and then they
all jumped to
the side…

Suddenly the
sun set. There
was a bright flash

and silver sparkles rained down from the air.
"What's happening?" cried Princess Aurelia
in astonishment.

Lila smiled and ran forward to clasp her
hands. "It's your happy ever after!" she said.

The music rose in volume. The White Cat
hugged Holly. "We did it! We stopped the
Wicked Fairy!" Holly laughed with delight.
All around her were happy laughing people,
dancing. Prince Florimund was swinging
Aurelia round. Lila was dancing with
Bluebeard, the King and Queen were joining
in too. Holly had never known anything like
it. The White Cat swung her back into the
dance. "So are you glad you stayed and
helped?" he cried as they skipped joyfully
together.

"Oh yes!" exclaimed Holly. It seemed strange now to remember that she hadn't wanted to, and just at that moment she felt her feet tingling. She looked down. Her shoes were glowing. "I must be going back," she gasped. "I will come here again, won't I?"

The White Cat nodded. "And I'll be waiting to meet you when you do. We're friends forever now!"

Friends. The word rang through Holly's head.

The last thing she saw was everyone waving and smiling at her and then a cloud of bright colours surrounded her and she whirled away.

An Apology

Holly landed in her bedroom. "Oh my goodness," she breathed. "I'm back."

Her eyes flew to her clock. She felt like she had been in Enchantia for hours, but just as the White Cat had promised, no time had passed here at all.

She sank down on the floor. "You really are special," she murmured to the shoes as she took them carefully off. "Thank you for taking me there!" Shutting her eyes, she relived the last minutes before she had left. The amazing dance, seeing everyone so happy, watching everyone smiling at her and waving her off, and then looking into the White Cat's green sparkling eyes as she was whisked away.

I've got a friend, she thought, *hugging herself. A real friend.*

She felt a pang and realised that she was really going to miss the White Cat now that she was back in the real world.

As she got changed the doorbell rang downstairs and her aunt called up to her. "Holly! Someone's here to see you."

Holly went halfway down the stairs and

found Chloe standing in the doorway. Holly stopped dead. She'd forgotten all about her ballet class and the row.

Chloe looked uncomfortable. "Um. You dropped this from your bag, Holly." She held out one of Holly's pink ballet shoes. "Madame Za-Za asked me to call by with it because I only live a few streets away."

Holly's aunt took it. "It was kind of you to walk round with it," she said. "Would you like to come in for a while?"

Chloe shook her head abruptly. "Thanks, but I think I'll head off."

"Wait!" The word burst out of Holly. She hurried down the rest of the stairs. Still glowing from her adventure, she wanted to make amends. "Um… thanks." She felt herself blushing. "Thanks for bringing my ballet shoe round. It was really kind of you."

Chloe looked stunned. "That's all right."

"Maybe… maybe I could walk back with you to your house," Holly suggested hesitantly.

Aunt Maria smiled warmly. "That's a good idea."

Holly held her breath. She wouldn't blame Chloe for saying no, but suddenly she knew she really wanted her to say yes.

Chloe paused, but then to Holly's relief gave a tentative nod. "OK."

The two of them left the house. "I'm sorry about how I acted earlier," Holly apologised. "I was in a really bad mood. I shouldn't have said those things."

"It's OK," said Chloe awkwardly. "I just thought you might want to be friends."

"I do!" The words came out before Holly had a chance to think. "If… if you still want to of course." She gave Chloe a hopeful look.

Just then, a gust of wind blew through the branches on a nearby tree. A cloud of leaves fluttered down, catching in their hair. Their eyes met and they both giggled suddenly.

Chloe face relaxed into a grin. "Come on, my house is this way!" She twirled round happily in the leaves. Holly laughed and joined in.

The two girls spun down the street together, the golden leaves decorating their hair.

Darcey's Magical Masterclass

Pas de chat

This lively move means 'step of the cat' because it's light and quick - just like a cat.

1.
Lift your right leg
to the side, pointing
your toe and
bending your knee.
Place your pointed
toe just above your
left knee.

2.
Hold your right arm out in front of you and your left arm out to the side at shoulder-level. Then bend your left knee and jump lightly into the air.

3.
As you jump, swap legs so that your left knee bends as your right leg straightens.

4.
Land gently on your right leg with your left leg coming down afterwards and in front. Repeat steps.

Magic
Ballerina

Holly and the Silver Unicorn

In Enchantia, Holly discovers a carousel of enchanted creatures, trapped on the ride by the Wicked Fairy. And there's just one more she wants to capture...

Read on for a sneak preview of Holly and the Silver Unicorn...

"I'm so glad to see you!" the White Cat cried. "Oh, my shimmering whiskers, Holly! This is the best surprise ever. You're bound to be able to help!"

"Why? What's going on?" asked Holly.

"It's the Wicked Fairy again," the White Cat said, his usually cheerful face looking suddenly worried.

Holly shuddered as she pictured the Wicked Fairy with her hooked warty nose, black wand and long cloak. She'd met her in her first adventure in Enchantia, when she'd tried to spoil Princess Aurelia's wedding anniversary. She was one of the few really horrible characters in Enchantia. "What's she been doing?" Holly asked.

"I'll show you!" The White Cat waved his long fluffy tail once and then used the end to draw a circle on the ground. Sparks shot up into the air and a mist formed inside the circle he'd drawn.

As the mist cleared Holly saw a carousel – a black iron merry-go-round with a spiky top. It was in the grounds of a dark creepy-looking castle and had some amazing creatures on it – a giant swan and dove, a magnificent stag, a brown bear and a sea dragon. There was one empty space left.

Holly looked at the White Cat. "That's the Wicked Fairy's Castle, isn't it?"

"Yes. And it's her carousel. She has been collecting all the most amazing creatures in the land and putting them on it."

"So they're real animals?" said Holly looking at the lifeless carousel creatures with their blank, staring eyes.

The White Cat wrung his front paws together. "Yes. They were all free to move about until she enchanted them. At the moment the magic is only temporary, so they could come back to life, but when the Wicked Fairy fills the final space, the magic will become permanent and then all those wonderful creatures will be lost forever..."

°ⓖ·*·☆·ⓖ·*·☆·ⓖ·*·☆·ⓖ·*·°

Hi, my name's Holly and I love ballet more than anything. Dancing makes me think of my mum because she's a professional dancer. I love the emotions and stories in ballet, sometimes I get so carried away I forget where I am! Luckily I'm always in the best places: dancing at Madame Za-Za's or in Enchantia The White Cat and I have done so much there: protecting Cinderella from an evil magician, reuniting Beauty and the Beast, and even making things right in the Land of Sweets!

Hair colour: Dark brown

Eye colour: Green

Likes: Expressing myself through dancing

Dislikes: Feeling left out

Favourite ballet: Sleeping Beauty (particularly the Rose Adagio dance)

Best friend in Enchantia: The White Cat

Magic Ballerina ™

Read all of Holly's adventures!

Magic Ballerina

Meet Delphie and Rosa too!

Magic Ballerina ™

Darcey Bussell

Buy more great Magic Ballerina books direct from HarperCollins
at 10% off recommended retail price.
FREE postage and packing in the UK.

Holly and the Dancing Cat	ISBN 978 0 00 732319 7
Holly and the Silver Unicorn	ISBN 978 0 00 732320 3
Holly and the Magic Tiara	ISBN 978 0 00 732321 0
Holly and the Rose Garden	ISBN 978 0 00 732322 7
Holly and the Ice Palace	ISBN 978 0 00 732323 4
Holly and the Land of Sweets	ISBN 978 0 00 732324 1
Rosa and the Secret Princess	ISBN 978 0 00 730029 7
Rosa and the Golden Bird	ISBN 978 0 00 730030 3
Rosa and the Magic Moonstone	ISBN 978 0 00 730031 0
Rosa and the Special Prize	ISBN 978 0 00 730032 7
Rosa and the Magic Dream	ISBN 978 0 00 730033 4
Rosa and the Three Wishes	ISBN 978 0 00 730034 1

All priced at £3.99

To purchase by Visa/Mastercard/Maestro simply call
08707871724 or fax on **08707871725**

To pay by cheque, send a copy of this form with a cheque made payable to
'HarperCollins Publishers' to: Mail Order Dept. (Ref: BOB4),
HarperCollins Publishers, Westerhill Road, Bishopbriggs, G64 2QT,
making sure to include your full name, postal address and phone number.

From time to time HarperCollins may wish to use your personal data
to send you details of other HarperCollins publications and offers.
If you wish to receive information on other HarperCollins publications
and offers please tick this box ☐

Do not send cash or currency. Prices correct at time of press.
Prices and availability are subject to change without notice.
Delivery overseas and to Ireland incurs a £2 per book postage and packing charge.